Coal Country
Christmas

by Elizabeth Ferguson Brown

illustrations by Harvey Stevenson

Boyds Mills Press

Text copyright © 2003 by Elizabeth Ferguson Brown
Illustrations copyright © 2003 by Harvey Stevenson
All rights reserved

Published by Boyds Mills Press, Inc.
A Highlights Company
815 Church Street
Honesdale, Pennsylvania 18431
Printed in China

Publisher Cataloging-in-Publication Data (U.S.)

Brown, Elizabeth Ferguson.
Coal country Christmas / by Elizabeth Ferguson Brown ; illustrated
by Harvey Stevenson. — 1st ed.
[32] p. ; col. ill. : cm.
Summary : A child's trip to her grandmother's house located in a coal-mining region results
in a memorable Christmas.
ISBN 1-59078-020-5
1. Christmas — Juvenile fiction. (1. Christmas — Fiction.) I. Stevenson, Harvey. II. Title.
[E] 21 2003
2002117183

First edition, 2003

Book design by Edward Miller
The text of this book is set in 16-point Pabst.
The illustrations are rendered in acrylic.

Visit our Web site at www.boydsmillspress.com

10 9 8 7 6 5 4 3 2 1 hc

For my grandmother, Elizabeth Loftus,
my mother, Elizabeth Ferguson,
and my family, who have always believed

—E. F. B.

To Leo and Jack

—H. S.

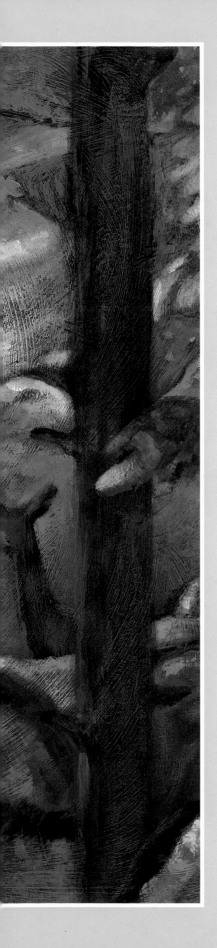

Along the road, black as coal,
we snake our way up and into the mountains.
Snow-topped evergreens
tower above us.
Soft-eyed deer turn their heads
as if to ask where we're going.
We're going home.
Home to the mountains of Pennsylvania
where my mother,
and her mother before her, were born.
Home to coal country for Christmas.

Smoke, dark with soot,
sends out its welcome
from coal country chimneys.
We watch it drift down
upon row after row
of heavily weathered houses.

The brightness of these homes
comes from within.
Yule trees, garlanded and glassed,
glimmer from parlors.
And grandmothers with silvered hair
wait patiently at frosted windows.

Soon I am swallowed up
in grandmother arms.
Home at last.

Few things change
in coal country.
The old stove is still there,
filled with hot,
shimmering coals.

My grandfather's empty rocker
sits by the window
where the sun used to gleam
on his whitened hair
a long time ago.
The lung sickness that comes to those
who go deep into the mines day after day
has left many empty rockers.
Coal country is not easy.
But we're here.
Here where we belong for Christmas.

In the cool front parlor
the yule tree gives off a warmth
that reaches down
deep inside me.
Old family ornaments
nestle comfortably among branches
as if they hadn't spent the year
tucked away in tight boxes,
impatiently waiting.
Behind me the kitchen rings
with motherly voices,
teasing, scolding, and above all, laughing.
Too soon the chatter dies down
and settling in begins.

I snuggle down in the soft, warm bed,
my mother on one side,
a place for my grandmother on the other.
My grandmother laughs her soft laugh.
She calls it the bed of the three Lizs
since we all share the same name—
my grandmother, my mother, and me.
In the light from the window

I see her standing before the old bureau.
Slowly she pulls the thin silver pins
from her hair.
I watch the neat tight bun uncurl
and the long twisted braid stretch down,
reaching to her waist.
Each year it seems a little longer
and a little grayer.

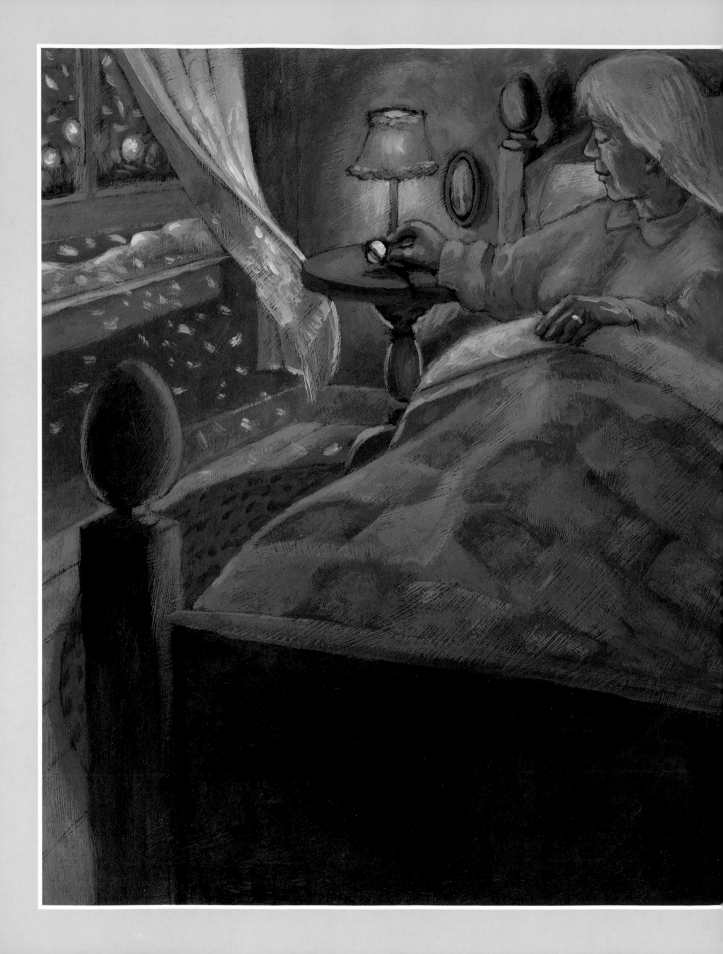

I watch her stop to open the window
just a crack.
When coal stoves burn
and mines run deep beneath houses,
gas can travel on silent feet.
But coal country families
learn to live with coal gas,
raising windows
even in winter.
The cold night air
creeps across the room to find me.
And if the silent snow steals down on us
as we sleep,
we are snug and safe
together.

Nothing sounds quite like coal
being shoveled into a hungry stove
or feels as shockingly cold
as linoleum on bare feet,
especially on Christmas morning.
We huddle together around the stove,
sharing its warmth.
At church we sit close
and enjoy the sweet feeling of being together.
In crunchy snow we walk home,
my hand tucked inside my mother's pocket.
My grandmother's legs move slowly,
but we are in no hurry.

Winding streets bring us past sights
all too familiar to coal towns.
It has been years since the mines closed,
but their mark is still here.
Houses and streets tilt
as old shafts collapse
beneath them.

Smoke rises from mines that smolder

even now.

And in the cemetery,

the row of headstones grows ever longer.

But families draw comfort from

those who are here.

And no one talks about the mines at Christmas.

Relatives laden with babies and bundles
crowd into the tiny house
until it is swollen with family.
Kissing and hugging make the rounds;
no one escapes.
Children are measured, pictures admired,
and treasured stories retold
again and again.
Stories of fathers and uncles
and grandfathers.
And if we are mostly a family
of mothers, sisters, and aunts,
it is not unusual
in coal country.

Using the ends of her apron,
my grandmother swings back
the heavy oven door
where the sizzling turkey hides.
From stove, icebox, and pantry
comes a parade of favorite dishes.

Finally, the room grows quiet.
The voice of my grandmother
drifts down the length of the table,
giving thanks for food,
and Christmas,
and family.

All too soon empty dishes disappear;
and just as quickly,
tea and coffee take their place.
But the best is still to come.
Months ago, candied fruit was diced,
mixed, and baked in a recipe
known only to my grandmother.
Lovingly she wrapped the fruitcake
and laid it away, to wait.
It is her gift to us at Christmas.
Though it seems more
than her swollen fingers are able to do,
a coal country woman does
what needs to be done.

Warmed by laughter, hugs,
and family,
we snuggle back in bed
once again.
In the quiet
I hear the rhythmic sound of the faucet
left dripping so water pipes won't freeze.
And the gentle swing of my grandfather's rocker,
as the dog curls round and settles down.
And finally, as I drift off,
I hear the sad, lonely wail of a train whistle.
Its cry echoes off the mountains
as it races against the night
leaving coal country behind.
Just as we must leave
in the early morning light.

But with us go memories
safely tucked away against days
far from coal country.
And I hold tight to each and every one—
that long, silvered braid in the moonlight,
my grandmother's soft laugh.
Content, I burrow down deep
in the bed of the three Lizs,
wrapped in the warmth
of a coal country Christmas.